School Cool Days!

CONTENTS

The School Cats

WRITTEN BY JEANETTE CUNIS

ILLUSTRATED BY JENNIFER COOPER

Peppy and Danny are our school cats. Peppy was born in the shed at the back of our school 16 years ago.

Her wildcat mother took
her other kittens and left Peppy
all alone. Peppy was very tiny, and
her eyes were not even open yet.

Our teacher took Peppy home.
She had to use an eye-dropper
to feed Peppy special milk.

When Peppy was older,
she followed our teacher to school
every morning. Every night, she
followed our teacher home again.

When Peppy was only seven
months old, she had one little
grey-and-white kitten.

Our teacher named the kitten
Annie, but the kitten turned
out to be a boy. So his name
is Danny!

Peppy didn't want to stay home
with her kitten. That meant
our teacher had to take Danny
to school every day so that
he could be with his mother.

Danny is grown up now,
but the cats still come to school
every day. They sit in the sunny
spots in our classroom.

11

This week, we had a party for Peppy's birthday. We think she's 112 in cat years. Wow!

For the party, we made colourful party hats and wrote poems about Peppy on balloons.

Our teacher made a cat-food cake with a cat candle on it.

Peppy got a big basket, two toy mice, and two cans of cat food for her presents.

Our class sat in a big circle
with the cake in the middle.
When Peppy came into our
classroom, she sniffed the cake
and then started to eat it.

15

Everyone laughed and laughed,
then we sang "Happy Birthday".
Everyone, especially our teacher,
hopes Peppy will live for ever!

Making Candles

Written by Jeanette Cunis
Illustrated by Jennifer Cooper

19

Soon it was going to be Mother's Day. Our class decided to make candles for our mums.

We put some wax and crayons into a bowl and melted them in the microwave. Then our teacher poured the mixture into dishes.

We had to hold a piece of wick in every dish of melted wax.

As we waited for our candle wax to set, Jason said, "Gee, my arm is getting tired."

Our teacher said, "I wonder what it's like working in a candle factory. Do hundreds of people have to stand around holding the wicks while the wax sets?"

23

We didn't know the answer,
so we decided to write to
a candle factory to find out
about candle making.

We found the address
of a candle factory on a box
of candles. Later that day,
we all wrote to the candle factory.

We asked all sorts of questions.
We also told them a little about
ourselves. Then we posted our
letters to the candle factory and
waited... and waited... and waited.

Two weeks later, a great big box arrived at our school. We were all very excited! We eagerly watched as Jason unwrapped the box.

Inside it, there was a book with photographs of people working at the candle factory. The book told us how candles are made.

There was also a candle
for everyone in the class.
There was even one for our teacher.

We read the book during reading time. Then, during writing, we wrote letters to thank the candle factory for our candles!

FROM THE AUTHOR

Peppy and Danny are real! When I was teaching, they used to sleep on my table at school. One day, we made candles and a birthday cake for Peppy. Then we put one of our class-made candles onto her cake.

Jeanette Cunis

FROM THE ILLUSTRATOR

I love to put cats in my stories. They can do funny things when the other characters aren't looking. My two cats like to sit on my paper as I draw. If their feet are dirty, I have to paint out their footprints with white paint!

Jennifer Cooper